· A
FINE
WHITE
DUST ·

Cynthia Rylant

A YEARLING BOOK

Published by
Dell Publishing Co., Inc.
1 Dag Hammarskjold Plaza
New York, New York 10017

For information address: Bradbury Press, An Affiliate of Macmillan, Inc., New York, New York.

Yearling ® TM 913705, Dell Publishing Co., Inc.

ISBN: 0-440-42499-2

RL: 4.7

Reprinted by arrangement with Bradbury Press, An Affiliate of Macmillan, Inc.

Printed in the United States of America

December 1987

10 9 8 7 6 5 4 3 2 1

CW

To Dick, for help
To Dawna and Diane, for friendship
To Gerry and Nate, for everything.

Contents

Dust

I've got these little bitty pieces of broken ceramic in my hands, and some of that fine white dust is coming off them, like chalk dust. There are some flecks of green paint on a few of the pieces. And some blue here and there. You'd never know to look at it that this mess used to be a cross.

I've been trying to forget it, keeping it in a paper bag in my bottom drawer for nearly a year now —since the summer of seventh grade.

But here's June again. Another summer ready and waiting for me. And old Rufus just itching for us to get into something.

I guess it's time to throw this mess away.

So if it's time, how come I still can't do it? How come I pour these pieces on my desk and look at them and roll them in my fingers and can't bring myself to chuck them?

I figure it's got something to do with finishing things up. Maybe if I just tell the story, tell it all from start to end, I'll finish it. Tell it right to the end, then chuck these pieces. Chuck this cross and put the Man to rest.

❖

Before last summer, before the Man ever came to town, I figure I was getting ready for him. I bet I was even getting ready in first grade, when I threw up all over Billy Winfred in Sunday school.

I guess I was getting ready for him all those years, those years I was loving church. I can't say why exactly, but I loved church from the start. My folks were never much interested, which makes it all the harder to understand why I was. When I was little, they'd take me to services now and then—like the day I threw up—but mostly on Sundays they just stayed home. And in our little North Carolina town, where the Baptist church is the biggest building of them all, with the Methodist second, it gets noticed when you're not a churchgoer.

But my folks went right on staying home and reading the Sunday paper all morning, just popping into church every now and then for Easter or Christmas. Never once fearing the wrath of God.

What was happening to me inside, I can't say exactly. But I didn't want to stay home Sunday mornings. So when I was in second grade, I just invited myself to go to church with the Fosters, who lived next door. Then about fourth grade, I started going on my own. Mother and Pop must have thought me slightly touched, but I went on anyway. And when I'd come back after services they'd say, "How was church?" and I'd say "Fine" and they'd say "Good" and that was that.

I guess it was sometime during fifth grade that I got more serious about church. I don't know why, but some part of me just got religious and there's no other way to explain it.

I remember one Sunday that year, I got to church kind of early and slid into the middle of a pew, waiting for the place to fill up. I was looking around, trying to act like I'd really meant to be early, when my eyes stopped on this picture of Jesus. I'd seen it before, but never really looked at it.

It was a big one, up behind where the choir sat. Jesus was wearing the crown of thorns, blood dripping down His head, and His heart was showing, like one of those pin-on hearts. It was bright red and glowed like it was burning.

And His eyes. They were like those brown ponds you sometimes see in the woods. So dark and shining—but when you try to see yourself in them, you can't. You look, and maybe you see a shadow of your head, but you don't see you.

I sat there that morning, looking up at that picture of Jesus, and I liked Him. I started liking Him that morning and I've never stopped. I can't figure it out. Before I was ever taught heaven and hell with any understanding of it, I liked Jesus.

And I liked Him so much that I guess as I got older, I got afraid of hell just because of Him. Those preachers telling me *He's* going to come back to judge me, *He's* going to cast me out, *He's* going to send me to hell.

Lord have mercy.

Why, the thought of standing there and having Jesus look at me, then point His finger away, just

6

point me right away from Him . . . the thought shook me to my toes. *Please*, I could see me begging Him. *Please. I like you.*

I didn't want to go to hell. I wanted somebody to tell me I wouldn't go to hell. I'd look at me and I'd see a boy who never did seem to be good or holy or worth anybody dying for. Just nothing real special. And I guess I wanted somebody to make me better. To save me from hell.

So last year, last June, somebody came to town who I thought could do that. I called him Preacher Man.

It's him I've got to finish up. It's him in these pieces of broken cross.

So I'm going to tell him to the end. And then I'm going to throw away every last piece of this cross, and I'm going to wipe my hands clean of that fine white dust.

2

◇

The Hitchhiker

It seemed like he came to town just for me. This man full of The Word, with The Power and The Light shining all around him. What was it, what was it, that made him come after me?

The first time I saw him, he was hitchhiking out on the 19–21 bypass. We didn't pick him up, so you'd think I wouldn't have noticed him, but he wasn't any ordinary hitchhiker. I was sitting up front, next to the window, and as we passed —going slow, because the road's nearly all uphill—he looked me right in the eyes. I could see that his were light blue (now, how many hitchhikers do you pass and know what color their eyes are?) and he was looking right at me. It was powerful. Scared me good. And those few seconds I thought I was looking into the eyes of a crazy man.

The second time I saw him was a few days after, on June 11. I remember because it was the last day of seventh grade and we got to go home early, so I went into town to loaf around. Hadn't been free on a Thursday afternoon for nearly a year. I wanted to soak it up.

He was in the drugstore. I'd gone in to look at comics, and while I was squeaking around the old rack to find some Fantastic Four, I looked over and *bam*, there he was.

I mean, he was there like a small *explosion*. Leaning against the counter at the soda fountain, hands in his pockets, sort of a ghost in a blue suit just *swallowing me up*. I knew those blue eyes, those hitchhiker eyes, and my heart flopped like a dying fish.

I looked at him for only a split second, then I scooted around behind the rack and buried my face into the first comic I could grab. It was a Baby Huey, and I guess I looked like a fool standing there reading it, but that big fat duck saved me.

Saved me.

I waited for the man to leave, but he stayed and stayed at that counter like a piece of hard rock. Darlene Cook had put his hamburger and drink down in front of him, but he still didn't sit down to eat. All this time I'm thinking he's some lunatic who hitched into town to murder people with a pickax, and I'm his first target. Darlene maybe his next. And I dug further into Baby Huey.

Then, like the Lone Ranger riding in, Rufus walked through the door. The bell tinkled as he opened it, and when I saw him, it was like a mighty chorus of angels just sang a few notes.

Rufus. You old sucker.

"Hey, Pete!" Rufus yelled when he saw me. The hitchhiker's head turned toward him. "Hey, you old hound dog!"

I stuck Baby Huey back in the rack like a hot potato and waved Rufus over. I slapped him on the back and made a couple of jokes and told him I'd buy him a chili dog at the truck stop, which got us both out of the store fast. As we were leaving, I never looked right at the hitchhiker, but I knew he had his eyes on me.

I didn't mention it to Rufus that day. Never mentioned that I'd likely be pickaxed before the summer was over. Rufus had too much sense than to listen to such stuff.

We'd been friends since kindergarten, Rufus and me, and two boys were never more different. From the day he was born, Rufus was a practical boy. He was popular at school, and I always figured it was because he was so honest and so practical. You could always trust Rufus to tell you what was what.

In fifth grade Rufus declared himself a *CONFIRMED ATHEIST*, and he's been that way ever since. For Rufus, the world you see is all there is. He wouldn't have any of that Spirit of the Holy Ghost.

We were so different, you'd wonder why we stayed best friends. But I guess I gave Rufus something to marvel at, with my spiritual notions and all, and I guess he gave me something solid to count on. The whole world might be a question mark, but Rufus stayed a good hard period.

So it helped, that afternoon, being with Rufus. We had our chili dogs, then we rode over to the volunteer firehouse to sit out front and eat a bag of pork rinds and split a Coke. You could watch the town passing by, sitting in front of the firehouse, and we liked that.

Rufus was telling me about the wrestling coach.

"Says I'm too cocky," said Rufus.

"You are."

"I'm not cocky, I'm *confident*."

"You strut it," I said, starting to laugh.

His lips spread into that smirk he was famous for.

"Well, when you've got it . . ." he answered.

"Strut it!" we both yelled.

We did some laughing that day. Rufus really wasn't cocky. In fact, I'd say he was pretty humble. But Rufus always knew what he wanted and what he'd put up with to get it. I guess a few might see that as cocky. But I always saw it as strength, and I envied him.

Rufus was solid like a rock. And I was the Jell-O Man. Some pair.

After a couple hours with Rufus that day, I felt sane again. And I put the hitchhiker behind me.

If only he'd stayed there.

That June something religious was itching me, that's for sure, and it seemed like it got worse just when the Preacher came to town. There were posters all over for Vacation Bible School, and they'd been getting to me. I'd gone to VBS every summer till I turned ten. Even then I would have kept going, because I liked painting those little ceramic crosses, but it was not considered cool after fifth grade. My mother had my painted crosses hanging in the kitchen, which was nice of her, considering her lack of interest.

The posters ruffled me. And I couldn't figure why. I was going to church every Sunday as usual, so that should have been enough.

But I was wanting more. There was some kind of longing inside me. I must have thought Vacation Bible School could fill it, whatever it was I needed. But I wasn't about to go at age thirteen and lose what little dignity I had.

So when summer vacation started, I ended up taking it out on my parents instead. I started simmering inside because they wouldn't go to church with me, because they didn't seem to care about heaven or hell or their boy's needs for religion.

If they were religious like me, I'd think, then we'd be a real family.

Maybe if I'd been in school, all this thinking wouldn't have happened. But my days were free, except for mowing lawns around town, and before one week of summer vacation had gone by, I'd been ruffled by some posters, spooked by a hitchhiker, and I'd decided my folks weren't religious enough to suit me. That's what free time can do to you, I guess.

I was fed up, and I'd been out of school just about two weeks when finally it showed at home.

"Hell," Pop said, when he knocked over the jelly jar at breakfast Sunday morning.

"Thought you didn't believe in it," I mumbled.

Pop's eyebrows went up. A bad sign. I always figured God had eyebrows just like Pop's, and when somebody lied or stole or punched a person in the face, God's eyebrows went right up like Pop's.

"What's that?" Pop asked.

"Nothing." I reached for my orange juice. He grabbed my hand, Mother watching us both.

"It was something," he said. "Something real smart, I'd say."

I forgot the juice and just sat back, silent.

"You have some complaint for me?" he asked.

"No."

"You think I shouldn't say 'hell'?"

"No."

"Well, what *do* you think, Mr. Cassidy?"

I knew I was in trouble then. Pop never called me Mr. Cassidy unless I made him real mad. I couldn't figure why my one little comment (smart,

I'll grant you) riled him so. But I knew I'd better start talking my way out of it.

"I think . . . I think people in town are wondering why you and Mother never go to church with me."

Mother sighed and put down her fork. I knew this was turning into something, and I was scared. Talking about God has always made me nervous. Like if I don't quote Scripture, I'll say the wrong thing and be doomed. God listening and his eyebrows going up.

Pop said, "Does what people think bother you?"

"No."

"I believe it does," he answered. He leaned back and folded his arms. "Are you ashamed of your mother and me?"

"Walt . . ." Mother began, reaching for his arm maybe to stop him, but he raised his hand and silenced her.

"Well," he said, "are you?"

I stared at my plate. I felt lonely, real lonely. My stomach weighed a ton. This wouldn't be happening if we were all the same, I thought, if we were all religious.

"No, sir," I answered. "I don't know. I'm just mixed up, Pop."

He took a deep breath then and let it out. He sipped his coffee and gently set the cup back in its saucer.

"There's more to it than you can see, Pete," he said softly. "Things you might not understand."

I don't know why, but those quiet words sent a swarm of chills up and down my body. I knew that when it got right down to it, I didn't want to know their secrets, Mother's and Pop's. Something in me was saying, *Don't tell, Pop. Don't explain. Don't tell.*

Mother shook her head, looking him right in the eye. I think he would have told me things if she hadn't. But he caught her look and he gave it up.

Instead he said, "Peter, you go to church as much as you want. What we choose has got nothing to do with what you choose. That revival's starting up. Some young fellow's come to town to preach. Maybe you need a good revival meeting. And if we don't, Peter," he said, looking straight in my eyes, "that's our business. Our souls are not for *you* to save. Do you understand me?"

I nodded hard and looked at Mother. Her face was sad and dark, and I worried for those seconds that she might die. I was frightened she might die and I could feel my breath getting small. And I didn't know if I was afraid she'd die because I didn't want to be without her or because I feared more than anything that she might burn in everlasting fire.

I never thought I'd go to a revival meeting. I guess I always figured it was for hardened sinners that regular church couldn't save.

But I followed Pop's suggestion, and that evening I went to the first revival of my life. And after that, I stopped worrying so much about Mother. Because the Preacher Man got me that night. And then the only person I was afraid might not survive this world was *me*.

3

❖

The Saviour

It was hot that night. Steaming. And it smelled like every lady in the place was wearing Jungle Gardenia and every man fresh out of a steel mill. The building was one giant hornets' nest, droning and droning and droning, and at first I nearly headed back home. I mean, for me church was fried chicken at the picnics and a little holy softball and ceramic crosses. I wasn't sure about God all in a sweat. It scared me.

Unfortunately, I got stuck in the middle of a pew and couldn't get out. A woman was down at one end with a baby and all those bags that go with it. And a fat man was at the other end, his knees taking up every last inch of space. And the smell of Jungle Gardenia closing in, front and back. I was trapped.

We all stood up and sang "Bringing in the Sheaves," big Joanie Fulton pounding away on the organ like some butcher pounding at a piece of meat. I knew the song by heart, and I'd missed singing it, so I sang all the verses through without ever opening the hymnal. When it was done, I felt good. Up. Yes, I was rising.

Then Woodrow Radford, the assistant pastor, got up and started talking about the revival, how it came to be, what it meant to us all, why every church needed one. Woodrow had a voice like a lawn mower—that dull kind of sound—and I was getting bored and nearly ready to make the fat man get out of my way, when the revival preacher was introduced and he stepped out from behind the choir into the pulpit.

"Lord in heaven," I said. The people around me turned their heads. "Lord in heaven."

It was the hitchhiker. The pickax murderer. Oh, my heart just *stopped*. It stopped cold, I know it, and my mouth hung like an idiot's.

Those light blue eyes didn't belong to any murderer. They belonged to a preacher.

Preacher Man.

I never heard his real name that night. Things real, things solid—they were gone. The Preacher began slow, and I knew that voice when he started. I'd never heard it before in my life, but I *knew* it. And I leaned into it, yes I did, I leaned my body into it and I let him take me. I was hungry for The Word. I didn't know it till I got there, but yes, I was hungry, and he did know The Word. What did he say? I wonder now. What was it he said? Doesn't matter. Didn't then. But he had a way. And I could feel the tears coming to my eyes as he preached. Yes. And I could feel my heart ache and ache with the longing. Hungry. And I wanted to be holy. Preacher Man, make me holy, that's what I said. Make me a temple.

And the others must have felt it, too. The church swayed back and forth with the rhythm of his voice, and it was like so many migrating birds, turning into the east all at once, turning into the west, turning and swaying and watching for the stars. The Star. Yes, we wanted to find holiness that night. The diaper-bag lady and the fat man and me and all the rest. Praise God, we said. Holy Jesus, we said. Forgive, we said.

Forgive, forgive, forgive.

I wanted to be clean. I wanted to sparkle. I wanted to dance with the Preacher Man in the glory of the Lord.

That night.

Yes, he took us all, and when he was done, we were no longer ourselves. We were his, Preacher Man's, and the sweat running off him and the sweat running off us was proof of it. I thought I had been cleansed. I thought I had been saved. I thought I had come home.

And when I walked up to him at the end of the evening, up that long aisle to ask him—beg him —to judge me a sinner, I looked right into those light blue eyes and he knew me. Yes, his eyes changed, and he knew me.

He grabbed my wet hands, and he said, "Are you a sinner?"

"Yes," I sobbed.

"Do you want to be saved?" he said.

"Yes, praise God."

His hands went about my head.

"God bless you. You have been born again."

And I fainted.

4

◇

The Joy

I woke up at sunrise the next morning. At first my mind was all spinning and dancing, and I thought it had been a dream.

Are you a sinner?

Do you want to be saved?

You have been born again.

For those few moments, I thought it was a dream, and I marveled at it and I smiled at it and I gave a long, deep sigh and then, *then*, it hit me.

No dream.

You have been born again.

Praise God, I moved my lips, lying there. I mouthed it again and again. Praise God, praise God, praise God, *praise God!*

And the joy came *leaping* from my heart. I was full, I was full, I was FULL of the Lord! Preacher Man's face was right there. I remembered just how he looked, and oh yes, he did forgive me. Oh Lord in heaven, he had *forgiven* me. Oh my Lord.

I might be best friends with an atheist, I might have half-washed Christians for parents, I might be weak and afraid to speak out for Jesus, but I was *forgiven*. I had longed to feel *BIG* in the eyes of the Lord, longed to make Him proud, to be *with* Him. And finally I was.

I lay there with the tears coming, and I thought that I was safe. Oh, thank God, I am safe.

Not many times in my thirteen years had I felt such happiness. Moments as a little child, I guess, that caused my heart nearly to burst—some wonderful toy, the ocean, my mother coming home to me. Such moments as those I guess brought the joy. But they were far from my memory, and that morning, *that morning*, when I woke up saved, there was nothing to compare such a feeling to.

Nothing.

Of course, I remembered fainting, and I was

some embarrassed by it. But I was out only a couple of minutes, and I wasn't the only one lying there at the Preacher's feet. They were all around, fainters just like me. And church members lifting us up and shouting and singing as they wiped our faces and told us to wake up now in the glory of the Lord.

I had opened my eyes in the arms of a big woman covered with sweat and with tears, but behind her, there were those eyes of the Preacher Man. I looked into his face and my heart swelled like the rising sun, and I knew I loved him. I loved everyone and everything that moment, but mostly I loved the Preacher Man.

After the service, some folks gave me a lift home, and I was glad of it because I didn't know if my legs could have carried me.

When I got home, my parents were up, watching TV, and I wanted to run into the room and hug them and cry with them about it all. But there they sat, looking at nothing, really, and being people I hardly knew. So I just went on to my bed and collapsed, dead till morning.

I spent two hours thinking about the revival before I went on down for breakfast. Pop had gone to work at the phone company already, and I saw

Mother in the yard clipping weeds, so I got me a bowl of corn flakes and took it out to sit with her.

" 'Morning," I said, and eased down onto the grass near her.

" 'Morning, honey." She smiled at me, her eyes all squinty. "Did you sleep well?"

I nodded hard, my mouth all stuffed with cereal.

"Good," Mother said. And she went on clipping her weeds.

I kept eating, not wanting to say anything till I was sure how to put it.

"Any yards to mow today?" she asked.

"Nope."

"Do you and Rufus have any plans?"

"Nope."

She nodded and clipped. I ate some more. It was quiet.

Finally she said, "And how was the revival last night?"

I swallowed down a big mouthful and took a deep breath, and I said, "I got saved, Mother."

She stopped clipping and turned to stare at me. I gave a sort of goofy grin and waited.

It took her some seconds to let it sink in. I didn't know what she'd say, but I was glad she was alone when I was telling her. I don't exactly understand why, but I was glad Pop wasn't there. Mother and I would have been smaller then, if that makes any sense.

She smiled, not a big smile and sure not a sparkling one, but she gave me a little smile and she said, "Well, I'm glad for you, Peter."

She looked at me deeper then for a minute, and she smiled again, and this time she seemed to really mean it. She said, "I'm so glad for you, honey."

I just grinned and shrugged and sort of played the goof again. Then I said thanks. I meant thanks, too. And she went on with her clipping while I headed into town.

You know who I was looking for. I didn't even know his real name yet, but I sure wasn't afraid of him anymore, and I had enough of the night before still ringing in me to want more than anything to see him that morning.

So I went to the drugstore. And like it was planned by God himself, the Preacher Man was there.

But this time he was outside the store. He had a cup of something hot in his hand, and he was leaning up against the wall with it, looking around. He looked so fine there, I remember. Like a young drifter who'd come into town—tall, silent, ready to be a hero. But first he had to have his coffee.

I guess seeing him again set off something in me you might call fear. Yes, I was looking for him—I wanted to see him more than anybody in the world—but all of a sudden my heart got to pumping and my hands went all sweaty and I thought maybe I'd just better turn back home. I wasn't up to it. He was more than I could handle.

But he saw me, the Preacher Man, and he lifted his arm and smiled so big and waved me over. I pushed the pedals on my bike with feet that felt like two tons of lead, but I made it to him.

His face glowed.

"And how *are* you, this wonderful morning?" he asked, sort of motioning to the good weather around us.

I was nervous. I must have showed my whole mouthful of teeth when I smiled back at him.

"Just fine, Reverend. Really. Mighty fine."

His face showed that he knew just what kind of fine I meant.

He said, "It's a wondrous thing to wake up in heaven, isn't it now?"

I thought, Why, that's just the way of putting it. In heaven. Yes, he knew about it.

I said, "Oh, it's as good as heaven on earth can be, Reverend. It truly is."

He agreed with me. And he went on about it awhile: what being saved meant to a soul, how it changed every last little part of a person's life, and so on like that. I ate it up. These were the words I wanted to hear, words I couldn't get from Mother or Pop or Rufus. I wanted the Preacher to go on talking all day, he made the light inside me shine so.

But he left off talking salvation, and he bought me a soda pop so we could sit on the steps of the post office across the street just to talk regular. I told him everything. About Mother and Pop, about mowing lawns, about seventh grade, about me and Rufus. He listened. He listened to me talk better than anybody ever had. And laughed, yes, he found me funny time and time again, and it made me jump with surprise when he'd let go with this big, open laugh. He seemed to like me. I seemed to be making him happy, and as we talked, I would think for a second, This cannot be real. Those hitchhiker eyes were so clear and all lit up, and it was like a crazy nightmare, those hours I thought he was a pickax murderer.

"You are some thinker, Pete," he told me. "I

do believe you might turn into a fine preacher yourself."

That made me blush. Imagine me, the Jell-O Man, doing to a church full of people what he could do.

He told me about his preaching, too, about his travels the last three years, selling all his possessions, hitchhiking town to town to revival preach. People heard of him by word of mouth and left messages for him at other churches, asking him to come preach. They'd leave word of their revival dates and hope he'd hear of them, and they'd never know till about a couple of weeks before if he was coming. But I figure everybody thought he was worth all that waiting and wondering if he'd show. I sure thought he was.

He kept bringing up his Wild Days, too. It was like he just couldn't get loose of them. He'd say, "Holiness didn't come easy, Peter. My eyes enjoyed what the Devil could paint. He could make things sparkle, make a glitter that blinded." When he'd start a Wild Days story—"I was living in New Orleans and keeping time with . . ."—I'd stop him. Change the subject. Because I didn't want to know about those days. Just don't tell me, I thought to myself. I don't want to know. Don't tell me.

I guess I wanted to think he'd always been like he was when I met him.

We talked a good three hours that day. And I did learn his name—James W. Carson. He told me I could call him Jim, not Reverend, and I did, though in my head I called him Preacher Man.

Anyway, it's hard to explain what happened between us those three hours. But we both did a lot of talking—me more than him. And laughing —him more than me. And he was so fine there, in his blue suit and white shirt, his face sort of tan and his blue eyes all happy.

It was like the man who had watched me and Rufus go walking out of that drugstore a week or so back just never existed at all.

Never existed.

5

◆

The Change

I should have known Pop would be disappointed
in me. Oh, he tried to hide it, to pretend he didn't
care one way or another. But I could tell it really
bothered him that I went and got myself saved.

And that hurt me.

I knew what Rufus said was true, that it wasn't
any of my business how my parents thought about
God, but that didn't change the way I felt deep
down. And deep down, I wanted them to be like
me. Pop especially. Pop was always a hard nut to
crack—never could tell just what he was
thinking—but church would at least have given

31

him and me something in common. Without it . . . well, without it, he wasn't anything like me at all.

I knew Mother had told him about me that evening, the second night of the revival. I was planning to go to church—I wanted Preacher Man to set my soul spinning again—but at supper I could tell Pop was troubled, and that changed my mind.

Mother and Pop were so quiet, it was like somebody had died. I felt like a fool, because I knew they were both thinking about me and not knowing what to say. I sure didn't know what to say. Mother would look at me a second, her eyes all soft and sad, then she'd look away. She had left a brand-new Bible in my room that afternoon, so I knew she wasn't mad about my being saved, but then again, she sure wasn't jumping for joy.

And Pop. Pop just fiddled with his food. It wasn't like him. If one thing made Pop happy, it was eating. And we were having fried chicken, his favorite. But he just fiddled.

So we sat like that for a time. Then Pop said, so fast it made me jump, "Are they going to dunk you in the river?"

"I don't know," I admitted.

Pop nodded. He looked at Mother and she looked at me and I looked at the chicken.

Then all of a sudden, Pop grinned. He said, "Remember when your granddaddy was dunked?"

Pop's grinning made me grin.

"Yep," I said.

Pop chuckled. "Old man wouldn't take off his glasses. Preacher tried to take them off him, but nothing doing. Dad said if any angels were coming, he wanted a good look at them."

Pop thought a second, then grinned again.

"Took his hearing aid off, though. I guess he figured whatever angels came along wouldn't be worth listening to."

I laughed and Mother laughed and Pop chuckled.

It was like things had never changed.

Pop grew quiet again, though, and awfully sad. I could tell. I thought maybe he was thinking about Granddaddy. Maybe missing him the way I'd miss Pop if he died. Or maybe he was thinking about me. But the look on his face made me want to stay home. I hated to leave the house when he was sad.

So I hung around. We three sat on the porch and watched the cars go by, commenting on this piece of gossip and that. We were all careful not to mention the revival or my salvation, and I wondered when it was that I learned not to talk to my folks about certain things. I mean, when I learned to be careful around them. Was I six? Or nine? Was it just last year?

When did that change? I looked at them and wondered.

Pop decided to turn in early, and Mother followed him, so that left me sitting alone about nine o'clock. I felt so depressed about everybody, I decided to go on over to the church anyway.

The place was packed. By the time I got there, Preacher Man was calling people to be saved, and they were surely coming. I stood in the back of the church, the heat hitting my face and the sweat starting to bead up under my nose. I stood and felt like somebody who had just walked into a stormy sea, with the waves coming in hard and sudden and trying to take you away.

They were up there, the sinners, crying and wailing and hanging on to each other. Some had fainted already. Most of the choir was crying so hard they couldn't sing. Joanie Fulton, her heavy feet pumping and her eyeliner running over her fat cheeks, sobbed and pounded at the organ. The place rocked.

And he was in control of them all. He was walking through them, his face burning and his hands reaching out. He smoothed the gray hair of the old ladies. He hugged the women. He hugged the men. He held the girls like he loved every one of them. He held them longest because they cried hardest.

I watched him move through them all, and I knew there was nobody like him on the whole earth. I wanted to run up and be saved all over again. I wanted him to see me, to look at me. I wanted to be special to him.

The tears came up in my eyes as I stood there, singing with the church.

And in my heart, I prayed it would go on forever. I prayed it would always be like this. I prayed things would never change.

6

❖

The Telling

And now comes the telling. The telling of me and
the Preacher Man.

You know, things changed after that second
revival meeting. No way they wouldn't. Because
while Preacher Man sure hooked me on the first
night, the second night he reeled me in. After I
stood in the back of that church, watching him,
tears streaming down my face, he had me. I would
have died for him. And in some ways, I guess I
did.

The telling.

I went home that night and dreamed him through till dawn. Dreams of Preacher Man and his sweat and his face and him pulling me down the aisle, pulling me in and in and in. I woke up worn out, like I'd never gone to sleep at all.

I didn't even bother with breakfast. I just dressed and got on my bike and headed for the drugstore. I was determined to sit in front of it all day long if I had to, waiting for him. I just wanted to be with him.

Now, what happened to me that morning, I can't exactly say. But I was not myself that day. I know it, and all I can guess is that part of me was still in some dream.

Old Rufus. I hadn't seen Rufus in a few days, so he didn't know I got saved. Not that he would be surprised by it. Rufus knew that I was always thinking on heaven.

But what Rufus wasn't ready for was the new me. And the new me was sitting outside the drugstore that morning, waiting for somebody.

Only Rufus came along first.

When I saw him I thought, Shoot.

Rufus was coming and I wanted to get rid of him.

The telling.

"Hey, you old hound dog!" he yelled when he saw me.

The hound dog wasn't interested. I gave a limp little wave and sort of looked up at the clouds.

Rufus pulled in on his bike.

"Hey, Pete, what's up?"

I looked at him. He was like somebody I'd never even met, it was that strange. I was looking at Rufus and nothing was clicking. To put it plain, I wasn't the old hound dog anymore.

"Not much." I was still looking around in the air.

Rufus, like I said, was not one to waste time getting to the point. He dropped his bike and sat down.

"What's wrong with you?"

Still inspecting the entire atmosphere, I said, "Nothing."

Rufus made a face and punched me in the arm.

"Aw, come on, Pete. You think I'm stupid? What's wrong with you? How come you're sitting here so dopey?"

Dopey. I couldn't believe it. I'm trying to look mature, plus uninterested, and Rufus calls me "dopey." I wanted him gone.

"Nothing's wrong," I said, my voice telling on my nerves. "Just waiting for someone, is all." I looked down the street, arching my neck like a rooster.

"Who?" Rufus asked.

"None of your business," I said right back, and regretted it the minute I said it. In all our years together, I never had said that to Rufus. Never. And when those words came out of my mouth, it was a shock to us both.

Rufus was kind of speechless. His shoulders drooped and his mouth hung open and he just stared at me with that look he usually reserved for really stupid girls.

What was I doing on a morning in June, waiting for some preacher and throwing off Rufus and never really knowing what was happening to me?

Before he could get his words back, I took a deep breath and said to Rufus, "Did you know I got saved?"

I looked him in the eyes real quick, but he still had that dumbfounded stare going.

He leaned over closer to me.

"You what?"

"I got *saved*." I was getting annoyed. The Preacher Man wasn't coming and that worried me, and even if he did show, stupid Rufus was going to sit there and stare at me till kingdom come. My insides were bouncing all over the place.

Rufus sat back again. He shrugged his shoulders.

"So?" he said. "What's wrong with you now?"

"Nothing!" I sort of yelled. "I just thought you might like to know I got *saved!*"

Rufus looked at me, shaking his head.

"So now you're saved and you don't talk to people anymore? What is it, Pete?"

And before I could tell Rufus what it was, which I didn't really know anyhow, the Reverend James W. Carson came walking up the street.

Preacher Man.

I sat there with Rufus, not saying anything, just watching that tall figure in blue moving on up the street. Like he *owned* the street. Like he *earned* the street.

I figured he did.

I stared at him and Rufus stared at me staring at him, until finally there he was, in front of us.

He looked down at me and smiled. That did it. I forgot all about Rufus and just broke into this outstanding grin.

" 'Morning," I said, looking up.

" 'Morning, Pete," he answered. He had his

hands in his pockets, and he was all loose and comfortable. I wished I wasn't sitting down.

The Preacher's eyes went over Rufus, who was giving him a good hard look.

Shoot, I thought.

"Uh . . . this is Rufus," I said.

Preacher held out his hand.

"How are you, Rufus?" he said, all those perfect teeth showing.

Rufus reached for the Preacher's hand, and I mumbled, "This is the preacher who . . . I mean, this is Reverend Carson."

Now, Rufus was always practical. So straight off he asked, "You the one who saved Pete?"

They had stopped the handshaking, and the Preacher was looking down on us both. I felt real small, but Rufus, he could have been ten feet taller than the Man, the way he was acting.

The Preacher gave a slow kind of smile.

"Well, I guess I am, though most would say it was the Lord God Almighty who really did the saving."

Rufus looked at me, then looked back at the Man. Then he did a funny thing. He stood up. I hadn't thought of it.

"Where you from, Reverend?" he asked.

The Preacher glanced at me with a smile, like we had some secret between us, and I loved that.

He said, "Nowhere and everywhere. Lately I come from heaven."

I loved it. He was something. I was so proud of him, standing there, it was like I was showing off a thing I owned.

Now, I should have known hard-hitting Rufus wouldn't take such an answer. I should have remembered that about Rufus.

It's funny, looking back, just how quick the Preacher Man did rile up my best friend. Put those two together on the street in front of the drugstore, and it was like a tornado, hot air hitting cold and just plain getting out of hand.

Rufus leaned up against a light pole and crossed his arms. I'd seen him do that many times—he reserved it for folks he didn't like. In a way, it was his battle position, leaning and crossing.

I picked up on it. And panicked. I thought, Don't you blow this for me, Rufus. Don't you mess things up.

Rufus said to the Man, "I never met anybody from heaven." He gave a cocky little grin. "Or the other place either."

Preacher Man looked at Rufus, and I could swear his face started getting square. It got this set look to it.

He said to Rufus, "If you aren't careful, son, you might get the chance." His eyes stopped smiling and took on that powerful look. "You could get yourself a free trip to either place. One-way."

I sort of chuckled, trying to lighten things up, but it wasn't working. Something was going on.

"Have you been saved, Rufus?" asked the Preacher.

Rufus glanced at me, then back at the Man.

"No."

"Have you considered, boy, that you could burn in eternal hell fire if you die today?"

"No," Rufus answered, looking the Man right in the eye.

"Lord have mercy," said the Preacher. He looked down at me—I was still sitting—and said, "Don't be corrupted, Peter."

"Huh?" I said.

"Don't be pulled down by the devils you cannot save."

It took me a couple seconds to realize he was talking about Rufus. *Rufus!* Pulling me down.

"Yes, sir," I said. And when I said it, I knew Rufus was looking right at me like a person betrayed. I knew that.

Preacher Man looked into my eyes.

"Be careful, Pete," he whispered. And without looking at Rufus again, he walked into the drugstore.

I swallowed hard and stared at the ground. I missed him already. He was right there inside that building, and I was out in front feeling like my whole life was just one big empty box.

Preacher, come back.

Rufus stayed quiet, leaning against the pole and looking at me. He uncrossed his arms and straightened up. He waited. But I didn't have anything to say, I felt so dead.

Rufus walked over and picked up his bike. He got on and rolled over beside me.

"Pete?"

I was still staring at the ground. "Huh?" I said, real quiet.

Rufus waited a minute. Then he said, "I'll be seeing you."

And it was a long time before I even noticed he had ridden off.

7

◇

The Invitation

And on the third night . . .

The third night, I had to wrestle with my heaven and my hell.

The telling.

I moped around the rest of that afternoon, after Rufus rode off. The Preacher stayed in the drugstore the longest time. When I stuck my face to the window to see what he was doing, I saw that Darlene, standing with her apron in her hand, had him cornered, and I gave up on him coming out anytime soon. Girls never shut up once they've got somebody cornered.

So I moped. I felt this awful ton of rock in my stomach and seemed like nothing in the world could knock it out.

Except him.

I knew I'd feel worse if I hung around the drugstore waiting for Darlene to let him go, so I rode around town, thinking and moping. I remembered how I used to look for Pop when I went around town, watching for a phone truck, watching for a lineman up a ladder. From the time I was big enough to look up at the sky, I loved to see Pop up there at the top of the telephone poles. I thought he had a power nobody else had, being up there. And the older I got, and the more I knew about electrical stuff zapping you right out of this world, the more I saw Pop as a brave man.

I wanted to be like him.

He told me things, back then. I guess I was six or seven. He told me he wanted to be one of those doctors who go off in the jungle to heal ignorant people. He said he never was smart enough to be anything but a lineman, but that didn't change what he would have been if he'd had a choice.

He'd tell me that, and I'd wonder why on earth he'd want to be a jungle doctor when he could climb higher and risk more than anybody I knew.

That was Pop and me, when I was little.

But the summer I was thirteen, the day I biked and moped all by myself, I didn't look for a lineman. Or for a best friend.

I didn't want anything but to be with the Man. And I couldn't wait for night to come. The dark and the heat and the tears and the Man.

Mother cooked ham for supper, but I ate so fast I hardly tasted it. Dinner was set late, and the revival time was coming up, and I didn't want to miss a minute of it. Walk me through all the Jungle Gardenia in the world: I'd be there.

So supper was fast. Pop discussed chain-link fences with Mother, and there wasn't that gloominess settling in like the night before. I could forget them and eat, then run like the devil.

I knew I had him only two more nights. I knew Preacher Man would be moving on after the next revival night, and I was afraid that my heart would never again explode with the spirit of the Lord. Never again would he look at me like he knew me inside out, blood and bones and cells and soul. Never again would anybody look at me and know how I felt, on fire with the Lord.

Two more nights.

I got there a half-hour early and already the

place was nearly full. I found a seat close to the front, and when I sat down, I could feel my heart pounding *thump-thump-thump*, so hard and loud, I was nearly embarrassed thinking somebody might hear it.

The choir was still in back, getting on their robes, so I had a chance to think.

I looked up at the empty pulpit. And I pictured myself walking into it. Peter Cassidy, Reverend Peter Cassidy, come to preach.

I would look into everybody's face. I wouldn't miss one. I would stare into everybody's eyes and I would tell the people to *like* the Lord. I would point to that big picture of Him behind me and I'd have them liking Him. I'd have them wanting to be saved so they could get into heaven to sit with Him and hear His stories and know that there really is somebody in the world who is perfect. Who loves them always. Who never changes.

"Reverend Cassidy, you have a way. You have a gift."

Then I blushed. I'm no preacher, I thought. It's not in me. Nobody's going to faint from the glory into my arms.

I couldn't even convince Rufus. I'm no preacher.

I stopped thinking about it and just sat thumbing through the hymnal, silently singing all those familiar words to myself. It was nice to be in a place where I felt so close with everything.

Eventually Joanie Fulton came out and started up the organ. The choir began filing in, mostly gray-haired men and women. Seemed nobody young wanted to sing with them. I figured I wouldn't want to either.

The minutes dragged and my heart nearly pumped itself right out of my body while I waited for the Man.

And then he came.

And like before, he had us all. Came out, and before anybody knew it, he had us so close to him it almost hurt. Maybe that's why the tears came. It hurt so much and felt so good all at the same time.

People started going up as soon as he said, "Come." They went up there to him, and you could see they didn't care about a thing but having him touch them. My eyes were so full, I kept having to use my sleeve to clear them out. People in my pew were going up there, and I wanted to go, too. Like always, I wanted to go.

Then, when I was stepping out into the aisle so somebody could get by me and go up, I looked toward the back of the church and saw Mother.

She was near the very back, sitting on the far edge of a pew, like someone who has to leave early. I stood there in the aisle, and with all those people and all that crying, and with my eyes so filled up, still I saw her. And I believe she saw me.

I say I believe, because our eyes met only for a second. Then more people came by me—Elton Fletcher raising his arms up to heaven, Fleda Lilly holding a handkerchief to her face—and by the time they had passed me, she was gone.

Mother. For a few moments, I felt like I did when I was a little child. When she would leave me home with Pop or Granny and go out the door, and I'd say, "Mother, don't leave me!" The door would close and I'd cry and cry and cry.

Mother, don't leave me.

Why was she there? Was it really her? I never learned. I was afraid to ask her. And later, I was embarrassed by the thought of what she must have seen on my face.

I loved the Preacher Man. She was my mother and she would have seen it. She would have known I loved him.

So when I couldn't find her in the crowd, I turned back to the pulpit, back to the Man, and I said "Amen" when he said it. I said "Hallelujah" when he said it. My body shook with joy and emotion beyond telling as I watched him. It shook with pain.

At the end of the meeting, when the organ and the choir and the Preacher were silent, I was spent. Worn out. I was in a daze.

So when I walked out into the night air and, still trembling, got my feet moving toward home, I hardly had the energy to be surprised when he stopped me.

"Pete?" He put his hand on my shoulder.

I turned sort of slow and looked at him. We were on the sidewalk. The last of the cars were pulling out. Most everyone who was walking home had already gone.

"Huh?" Then I realized who it was. The happiness just broke loose over my whole body, and I smiled at him.

"Hi, Reverend."

He sighed and smiled, almost sadly, pulled out a handkerchief, and wiped his face with it.

"A good evening of salvation," he said.

"Sure was." I stood fidgeting with my hands.

"I'm worn out," he said quietly, and I nodded my head at him in sympathy.

"I'm going to walk down to the pop machine at the filling station," he said, stuffing the handkerchief in the pocket of his jacket. "You want a pop?"

I said okay, and we started down the street together. Like I said, I was so tired I could hardly muster up the nervousness I usually felt when I was around him. So I was quiet and content, and we walked.

We got to the machine about six blocks down and took our pops to sit on the stone wall alongside the station.

He took the longest drink of root beer I ever saw a grown man take. Then he wiped his mouth, stood up, took off his jacket, and sat back down.

Without his suit jacket he was like a stranger. For a minute I looked at him in his shirt, and he was nearly like any other man. That jacket did cast its spell.

"I'm worn out, Pete," he said softly.

I nodded my head again.

He looked up at the stars.

"When I was a boy," he said, "I had a friend named Johnny Mitchell. He'd been in the navy and he had tattoos and he brushed his teeth with baking soda."

I nodded, wondering where the Preacher was heading.

"Johnny never married. He lived with his folks and he drove coal trucks, wrecking one every now and then.

"And Johnny loved me. He bought me cheeseburgers and Juicy Fruit and he taught me how to swing on a grapevine."

Preacher looked at me with a sad smile.

"He drove a Rambler and tailgated everybody, and he cussed all the time." The Preacher took a deep breath. "But because of him, I grew up thinking I was safe."

Then the Preacher was quiet again. I didn't know what to say. But what came out was, "I always want to feel safe, too."

And I guess it was the right thing to say, because he looked at me like I'd said something important.

"I was always different, Pete," he said. "Not in an obvious way. But I knew I was different.

"When I was sixteen there was this boy in our high school. From Russia."

"Russia?" I said.

"Yes, sure enough. His name was Varas. He had owl eyes and round glasses and knew math like nobody's business. He played jazz saxophone and told great stories. But since nobody could pronounce his last name and since his family wasn't Christian and since he was just too smart for us all to keep up with, Varas was mostly alone."

I shook my head in sympathy for Varas and started to say he sounded like a great guy, but then the Preacher added, "Like me."

"You?" I asked. At first I didn't see his connection.

He smiled. "Alone."

He looked up at the sky. "Jesus Christ was fortunate. He had companions, disciples. Somebody to talk to."

When he said that, the night changed for me. It wasn't happy anymore; it was sad. And I knew: Preacher Man wasn't perfect. He was lonely.

Again I didn't know what to say. I just sat there, wondering how to make somebody like him feel better.

Then he spoke. "But I have my rewards." And as his face lit up, my heart sort of lit up with it.

"I've met more people and seen more things

than most men twice my age, Pete. I've been able to show people what's real and what isn't.

"And at night," he said, "at night, after I've been preaching, I lie down and my soul is ready to *explode*, the joy is so powerful in me."

He got up and started pacing around, the way he did at the revival meetings. He wasn't looking at me anymore. It was like he was talking to a big crowd of people, and his talk got faster and faster.

"I think about the faces I've held in my hands and the people who have fallen to their knees before me, and I feel like I *know* Jesus Christ, like I *am* nearly Jesus Christ himself!"

His face was getting broad with his joy, and I felt it, sitting next to him. Felt it like a current of electricity. I trembled inside, it was so strong.

"And you, Pete," he said, stopping in front of me. "I see it in you. I see the preacher in you, and it stirs me up inside."

"Me?" I said, pointing to myself.

"I see it in your face, Peter." He started pacing again, moving away from me. "You are busting out with the power of the Lord, and you don't even know it. You have a power to do things, to help. You could make the people fall down on their knees. You could . . ."

And he stopped, his back to me and his face looking down the road that led out of town. He stopped dead, and the silence was tight and heavy while he stood there, looking out toward something I couldn't see. And just when I was getting nervous and ready to make a sound, the Man turned around and looked straight at me. He looked at me and quietly said, "If only you could come."

"Come where?" I said.

"Into the world. See what I see. Save the lives of thousands of people."

He came back and sat down beside me, his head close to mine.

"I hate to see you wasted, Peter. A boy touched by the hand of God is a boy apart. Look at those around you—your parents, your friends. Are they not blind to the light that shines in you?"

He paused, then said more softly, "Are they not strangers to you?"

And the tears wanted to pour. I started to feel them when he said that, and they wanted to pour. But I held back.

He touched my arm and I could feel the heat of his hand through my sleeve.

The Invitation

"People will die and burn in hell if not for me, Peter." His eyes were wide and wet in the glow cast by the streetlamp. I couldn't look away.

"You can come with me and help me save them, Peter," he whispered. "You can come."

The tears stung, my heart pounded, my hands sweated, and my mind searched for reasons to say no.

"Will you come?" he whispered.

"Yes," I said.

8

❖

The Leaving

Thy kingdom come, thy will be done . . .

God's will was to have me travel with the Preacher Man. It was so clear to me that night, when he asked me to come with him, when I said yes, when we made our plans.

Thy will be done.

What were Mother and Pop to me, when the Lord was urging me to go? Jesus left his parents, didn't he? But he was lucky. They knew he was the chosen one. My parents didn't know that about me.

Thy will be done.

I sat there with the Man, next to the filling station, and we made plans till nearly eleven-thirty. I would have sat with him all night long, but I didn't want Pop out looking for me. I didn't want Pop coming after me.

We made our plans. I would meet him after the last revival meeting. I'd skip the meeting, since I'd have to bring my belongings. And we'd hitch-hike out of town.

In my dreams that night, I was always fixing to leave. All night long in my dreams I was ready to go, all set. Ready to leave. So when I woke up and found myself in my own bed, in my own room, I was surprised by it.

Leaving home.

You think about it now and then. If you could just get away, you could find what you want. If you could just light out on your own, you'd find out about life. You'd be free.

Thinking about home, that morning, and leaving it behind me . . . I tell you, I didn't know it would be so hard.

You love some things without ever knowing it. I never knew how much I loved the window beside my bed till that morning. Every day of my life I woke up next to that window. And if it was summer, the breeze would be coming through the screen and I'd hear the cardinals and the neighbors' old dog. On Saturdays I might hear Pop with the mower and smell that sweet smell of grass coming into my room. And if it was winter, there'd be frost all around the edges of the window and I'd lie there, looking at the sparkles and the crystals, digging deeper under the quilts and feeling good about things.

Never knew I loved that window so.

And there are things about a house you grow to count on. Like the way the pipes squeaked when Mother was in the kitchen, washing up some dishes or cooking. The smell of Pop's shaving cream still in the air when I hit the bathroom in the morning. The ticking of our big old clock on the mantel in the living room. The feel of our fat couch when I'd sink into it with a comic book. The garage, smelling of oil, with my bike there and Pop's tools hanging where they always belong.

Things you count on. Things being where they belong.

I woke up that morning knowing I had to leave it all to go with the Man, knowing I had to go, and still wishing mightily that I could take it all with me. Mother and Pop and the house and the street and the town. What kind of person was I going to be without it all?

In the evening, when I left with the Man, I would be without it all.

Still, I met the day feeling higher than ever. Because I knew that I would never, *never* have to be away from the Preacher. In three days I'd come to depend on him so much. I'd come to rely on him being there, speaking The Word, looking at me with eyes that knew things. And I just couldn't imagine how I would survive after he left town. I couldn't imagine just going ahead with my mowing and knocking around town with Rufus. And the thought of going back to church and looking up at that pulpit and not seeing the Man there— how could I survive it?

Well, I was going with him and I didn't have to worry about those things anymore. What I had to worry about was what to pack, what to write Mother and Pop in my good-bye note, and whether or not the Preacher and I could stay out of sight and get far enough away so the police wouldn't be dragging me back home.

But the leaving worries I left mostly to the Man. I knew he could take me with him. He had The Power.

Pop was at work and Mother was out that morning, so I had the house to myself while I gathered up some things to take with me. It was like God was giving me a hand, letting me have an empty house.

Every person in the world must think about what he'd grab if his house was on fire. What things he'd take with him as he was running out the door.

That's how I felt, trying to pick and choose the things to take with me. What was important? What did I need never to leave behind?

I walked through the house, looking at the family pictures on the wall: Mother and me sitting beside a big fat jack-o'-lantern. I was about three. Pop and me with our fishing lines in the river. I was about seven in that one. Me poking my head out of my backyard tent. I was about ten then.

I wanted to burn the pictures into my head, so I wouldn't forget.

But I made my choices. I took from one of our picture albums a photograph Aunt Sue took of me and Mother and Pop the last Christmas. And a picture of my dog who died a couple years ago. I took one of my little ceramic crosses off the kitchen wall. I took my award medals for Best Speller and Best Citizen from Mother's jewelry box.

And I put them into my duffel bag with as many clothes as I could cram in. The Preacher told me to travel light, so one bag was all I could take.

Besides, you can't stuff a bedroom window into a bag.

Then, when I was just zipping the bag shut, Rufus called to me from downstairs. If the screen door was unlocked, Rufus generally just walked on into the hall and yelled. It nearly made Pop's ears smoke, he'd get so annoyed. But Mother liked Rufus, and she told Pop, "Let the boy yell. He feels at home here."

So Rufus was downstairs calling my name.

At first I wanted to crawl under the bed and hide till he went away. I felt like I'd been caught at something, like I'd been doing something wrong and Rufus had walked in on it.

Then I felt the pull to see my old friend. Rufus had been the best friend in all the world to me, and I was sorry that he couldn't come with me or ever understand what it was between me and the Preacher. Rufus and I had gone our separate ways, that was clear to me, and there was nothing I could do to change things. Still, the old hound dog in me wanted to see him.

But before I could make up my mind what to do, he was walking into my room.

"Hey, Pete." He gave me a friendly knock on the arm and sat down on the bed.

"Hey, Rufus." Now that he was in the room, I felt stranger than ever. I didn't know what to say to a boy I'd been friends with for seven years.

He looked at my duffel.

"Going somewhere?"

"Clearing out some stuff," I answered.

Rufus nodded, then let his eyes wander around the room. He sat on the edge of the bed, his shoulders drooping, his arms dangling between his legs.

"So, whatcha doing today?"

I knew he would ask that. He'd always sit just that way on my bed and ask just that question when he was bored and looking for something to do.

I didn't know what to say. There was no way I was going to bum around with Rufus on my leaving day, but I never was a fast liar and I couldn't think of what to say.

I shrugged my shoulders.

"Want to go swimming?" he asked.

I shook my head. "No, I don't think so."

Rufus considered things a minute, and I stood with my arms crossed, looking out the window.

"Pete," he said, "you mad at me or what?"

"What makes you think I'm mad?" I was still staring out the window.

Rufus watched me.

"I don't know," he said. "Seems like you're trying to keep away from me or something. I've never seen you act so funny."

I flopped down in my desk chair.

"I'm not acting funny," I answered, trying not to look him in the eye. "I'm just . . . preoccupied is all."

"What with?"

"Oh, just . . . things."

"What things?"

"Things, Rufus, just *things!"*

My voice got too loud, and it made him jump. He stared at me.

"Well, hell, Pete . . ."

"Don't say that!"

"Say what?"

"You know."

"What? *Hell?*"

"Yeah. You ought to know better than to say that around me."

"Hell, I mean, *heck*, Pete, I've said it around you a thousand times."

"Not since I got saved," I answered. I don't know what was wrong with me. I guess I thought I was already some kind of assistant preacher and Rufus was my first sinner.

He screwed up his face.

"I figured so," he said.

"Figured what?"

He looked at me, and I could see he was getting hot.

"I figured that preacher had you crazy in the head."

That burned me. I jumped up and said, "What business is it of yours, anyway? Since when do you know it all?"

But Rufus wasn't stopping.

"He's got you crazy, Pete. Anybody can see it. I mean, it's like you're living on Mars the last few days. And when he walks up, you might as well be some robot, the way he's got you remote controlled. 'Yes, Preacher. No, Preacher. Let's get those devils, Preacher.' "

I was so mad I felt like smashing his face. First person in the world I ever wanted to hit. I wanted to cuss him out and I wanted to knock him out. And feeling that way, I was wondering all the time what the Lord must be seeing in me.

I tried to get hold of myself. I sat down hard on the chair again and clenched my fist, then un- clenched it. I took a deep breath.

"Rufus, you've got no idea what you're talking about."

"The hell I don't. Pete, what is going *on*?"

I sighed real hard and flopped my legs out in front of me. I never have been able to stay mad at anybody for long. Especially Rufus. I was al- ready tired of fighting.

"You won't understand," I said.

"Try me."

And I wanted to. I wanted to try him, to see if he would understand, because so much was hap- pening to me, everything changing so fast, I needed somebody to tell. My duffel bag was sitting there, full of my last thirteen years in that house with Mother and Pop, and I needed somebody to tell.

"I'm going with him," I said, real low.

Rufus leaned forward.

"With him?"

I nodded my head. "I'm leaving town with him. I've been called to help him preach."

Rufus's mouth hung wide open.

"Who called you?" he asked.

"*God*, you fool! *God* called me!" I couldn't believe how thick Rufus could be at times.

Rufus just stared at me some more. Then he asked, "When you leaving?"

"Tonight."

"Tonight?" He sat straight up. "You're just taking off, just like that? What about your folks?"

I was ashamed to look at him when I answered. "They don't know I'm going." I stared at the floor.

Rufus took some seconds to let it all sink in.

"Pete," he said, barely a whisper, "Pete, you ought not to do this. It's going to hurt them real bad."

I looked at him, exasperated.

"You think I don't know that? You think I don't know? I *know*, Rufus. I *know*. But there's nothing I can do. God has called me, and I can't turn my back. I've got to put God before everything else, even Mother and Pop. Call it screwy if you want. But I can't live any other way, Rufus. I just can't."

I was looking at him then, my best friend, right in the eyes, because I was telling the truth and I wasn't afraid of it. And I was begging him, I guess, begging him to forgive me and to understand. I needed somebody in the world to understand.

He didn't. I knew he didn't. But I figure he knew I was dead serious, and I figure he was willing to accept what I was telling him. So he didn't say anything more about my folks.

"Well . . . what time you taking off?"

"After the revival tonight."

"You just going to walk out of the church with him and keep on going?"

"We're meeting up at Anderson's filling station about ten. Then we'll head out of town."

"Your folks won't be out looking for you?"

"They'll think I'm cleaning up at the church till after midnight. By then, they'll both be asleep. Won't know I'm gone till morning." I felt ashamed telling him. "I'm going to leave them a letter, though. I'm going to explain."

Rufus wasn't looking at me anymore. He was looking at his feet and shaking his head. He didn't say anything for a long time. Then he finally stood up.

His eyes were out the window. Rufus couldn't turn his face to me.

"Well, Pete," he said, real quiet, "I guess there's

no talking you out of it." He walked over and stood a minute at the door.

"I'll look after your folks," he said.

Then he was gone. And I was left sitting there with all that shame.

9

❖

The Wait

Right about here I feel my insides hardening up, and I think the telling has got to stop.

Yea, though I walk through the valley of the shadow of death, I will fear no evil, for thou art with me. . . .

Yes. I have known that valley and that fear. I have known the shadow of death. And, in the remembering, in the telling, there is a terrible loneliness.

My best friend left me that morning with all the pain that comes to you when you hurt somebody you love. Rufus walked out, and I sat there in my room, thinking about Pop working on the lines, Mother's face when she saw me at the revival. Thinking about how much I owed them.

It's a terrible pain.

But even with the guilt, even so, unfortunately I still thought I was doing the right thing. You owe your parents for a lot. But you owe God for your whole existence. You owe Him for life everlasting. How can you turn your back on the One who made the heavens, and the earth, and *you*?

I could not turn my back.

I took my duffel outside and set it in the bushes behind the garage.

I spent most of the rest of the day working around the house, doing all those chores I'd kept putting off. I cleaned out the basement for Mother and I painted the light post for Pop. I mowed the yard and I pruned the hedge. I even gave the front porch a good scrubbing.

Just as the Lord would have wanted it, I set my house in order.

And the work felt good. I sweated and I strained in the heat, but it felt good, those hours when my hands were busy and my mind clear.

Later in the afternoon, Mother came home with the car full of groceries. Mother always liked to buy food "for her two men," she said. So when I helped her carry the bags into the house, there was this ache in me. And as we unpacked the stuff, and I saw my favorite cookies and the canned meat nobody in the house liked but me, the ache got so bad I thought maybe something really was wrong with me, and I wondered if somebody thirteen could have a heart attack.

When I was little, I remember I used to talk to Mother about what I'd be when I grew up. And the most important thing to me was that whatever job I had, she could be with me. I guess I couldn't take the idea of living by myself, without Mother. So I'd tell her we could both be scientists and have our own laboratory. Or I'd tell her I wouldn't have a job at all, but I'd just stay home with her and make toys to sell to people.

I really loved Mother, and being around her, and unpacking the food she'd bought for me that day really hurt.

When Pop came home we all had a quiet supper. I tried to look at Pop while he ate, without him thinking I was staring at him. Poor Pop. That's what I thought. Poor old Pop. I wished he'd had more chances in his life. I wished he'd gotten the things he wanted.

And now he had a boy who was going to walk out on him.

You hear about broken hearts all the time. I always turned up my nose at it, thinking it was some kind of girl talk. But looking at my two folks at supper that night, I could swear I felt my heart just cracking right up the middle.

And after supper, when I sat on the porch with Mother while Pop watched TV inside, I wondered why God had done it all to me. Made me meet the Preacher and set me on fire. Why God was calling me away from my folks. Why he couldn't find some way to let me have the Preacher and have them, too.

Most times I could see God's hand in things. But this time it seemed he was just looking the other way, leaving me with all the complications.

But I'd still go with the Preacher. I'd go with him because we were meant to be together, him and me. Because life with him would be the closest thing to heaven on earth. And because he needed me. He needed me more than Mother and Pop did. They had each other, but he was alone and carrying the burden of the sin of the world.

That was the thing about Jesus that got to me: how *lonely* He seemed. The last person on earth who should have been lonely. But He was the most alone person I ever could imagine.

I didn't want the Preacher Man to suffer like that.

I'd still go with him.

❖

Night came, and I told my folks I'd be walking over to the church about ten o'clock to help clean up. I told them a bunch of people would be there, that I'd get a ride home with somebody, not to expect me till after midnight. I said it all and even looked them in the eye and couldn't believe how easy that lying was for me.

There was a duffel bag sitting outside in the bushes, there was an empty space on the kitchen wall where a ceramic cross used to hang, and there was a new boy named Peter Cassidy, all set to go out into God's big world.

So about nine-thirty I went to the front door. Mother and Pop were still watching television. I stuck my head in the living room, and in a voice I didn't know could be mine, I said, " 'Night."

" 'Night, Pete," Pop called, never taking his eyes off the screen.

Mother turned her head toward me, though, and in that split second her face looked just the way it did when I saw her at the revival. I can't describe it. It was just a strange look I'd never seen on her any other time.

"Don't be out too late, Pete," she said in a quiet voice. My heart sort of stopped then.

"Okay, Mother. See you later."

And I smiled and lifted up my hand in a wave as I went out the door, with one giant sob buried deep in me and wringing me inside out.

I fished my duffel bag out of the bushes and headed for the filling station. The walk was about fifteen minutes, so I had plenty of time. I sure didn't want to risk being late and setting the Preacher all in a panic.

The night was cool and dry, the sky clear. While I walked, I tried to block out thoughts of what I was leaving behind me, like the way I used to block everything from my mind when I was learning to dive. I was scared to death, but I'd make my mind go blank and I'd walk out on that board and I'd be diving in before I knew it.

So I blocked out everything except a picture of the Preacher Man in my head, and I walked on.

The streets are nearly always deserted in town after nine o'clock—it's just that kind of place. As I got nearer and could see the station in the distance, it didn't surprise me that there wasn't a soul around. There hardly ever was.

I was a few minutes early, I knew, so I just walked on under the streetlamp and over to the wall where the Preacher and I had made our plans the night before. It seemed hundreds of years ago. I was nervous, and I thought about getting a pop just to calm myself down, but I changed my mind. He might come all in a hurry and I might not look right with a pop in my hand. I ought to look ready to bolt any second. So I just sat up on the wall with my duffel by my feet, and I waited.

There was a clock lit up inside the station that kept the right time. Five minutes to ten. Five minutes and he'd be coming up the street, walking so straight and nice, and he'd say, "Let's go, Pete." My body shook with nerves, and I wasn't even thinking of Mother and Pop and home.

I was ready.

When the clock hit ten, and I didn't see him coming up the street, my nerves got worse. But I knew anybody at church could still have him cornered, still be pouring out their sins to him. He wouldn't walk away from anyone in need. Even if it meant me having to wait for him. He had to minister to the needy first.

I was sitting there, wondering how the last night must have been, how many more sinners he had pulled up that aisle, when Joanie Fulton and her boyfriend came walking down the street.

I felt like I'd been caught at something and I panicked, but Joanie just smiled and said, "Hi, Peter." Her boyfriend ignored me.

I lifted my hand in a wave and tried to look casual, like I sat on that wall every night at ten o'clock.

"Good revival?" I asked, trying to sound not too interested.

"Great," she answered. "He fired up the whole place." She laughed. "I was crying so hard I couldn't see my music, so I squawked out more sour notes on that organ. . . ." She buried her face in her boyfriend's shirt, the way girls do sometimes, and giggled.

"Yeah." I half smiled. "Well, see you."

I watched them go off, thinking how lucky the Preacher was not to have a girl always hanging on him.

I figured he'd be along real soon, since Joanie had already gone.

The minutes kept on ticking by, and I wondered again about getting a pop, but I figured as soon as I snapped it open he'd come hurrying up the street. We were going to hitchhike all night long, and the later we got started, the harder it would be to get a ride.

"Come on, Preacher," I whispered to the air.

You think there aren't enough minutes in the day to do all you have to do sometimes. But watch a clock and those minutes go so slow, you wonder how anybody gets through a whole day with so much time sitting there to be filled up. I watched that clock's hands move so slow and I watched the street stay empty and I thought God had just hung me up in another time zone. I wondered if everything around me was real. The deserted station with one fluorescent light burning inside. The street all black and empty except where the poles left a puddle of light every block. The stone wall I sat on with my hands twisted up tight, squeezed between my knees. My duffel stuffed with my life, sitting on the sidewalk beneath me. And the clock just ticking and ticking and ticking away the empty, silent minutes.

I sat there on the wall, my eyes looking as far up the street as eyes could look, until eleven o'clock. Eleven o'clock and still no Preacher.

Must be an emergency, I told myself. Must be somebody in a bad way. He must be worried about me sitting here waiting for him.

Eleven-thirty.

I know there's some good reason, I told myself. Some good reason, but he just can't send me word. I'll wait on him. He'll be here.

Midnight.

I walked up and down in front of the wall, stopping to stare at the empty street. Once a car came by, but it just went on.

Some good reason, I told myself.

Twelve-thirty.

I got a pop. I drank it all down in one gulp, and I squeezed the can hard in my hand. I squeezed it hard as I could, then I threw it in the street. The noise made me shake but the throwing felt good.

One o'clock.

He's not coming.

I stood in the middle of the street, feeling so heavy, all of me so heavy, and I told myself the truth:

He's not coming.

And slowly I walked over to the wall, picked up my duffel, and slowly I started back down the road for home. I was a half-block down the street when somebody rose up out of some bushes, and my body gave one big jerk of fear and hope. Preacher, I thought.

"I'll walk you home, Pete," Rufus said.

Rufus. Old friend. I couldn't move. Just stared at him, thinking I was having some kind of hallucination.

"Come on, Pete," he whispered, putting his arm around my shoulders. "Come on and go home," he said.

And I never spoke a word. I just walked on, letting Rufus take me home, and never speaking or feeling or hearing or seeing anything real around me.

The fifteen minutes going to my house was like two. We went up the walk and Rufus swung open the front door for me. I stood there, not knowing what to do.

"Rufus?" I said.

"Go on in, Pete. He's not taking you. Go on. Go to bed."

Rufus guided me through the door.

I turned around and looked at him, my eyes so tired and heavy.

"Sure?" I asked.

Rufus nodded his head.

"Go on, Pete."

And I went on up the stairs while Rufus closed the door behind me. I went into my own room and lay down on my own bed and felt the breeze from my own window running over my face, as I closed my eyes and wished to die.

10

◆

Hell

Dear Mother and Pop,

Please don't be mad at me and don't be worried. My bed's still made and I'm gone because I didn't come home last night. And if you will read this letter real slow, you will find out what happened.

First, I'm sorry I had to lie to you both last night. There wasn't any other way.

I have left town with Reverend Carson. He's the revival preacher at church.

PLEASE DON'T WORRY. This is God's will for me and there is no safer place on

*earth than with Reverend Carson. He will
take good care of me and I'll eat right and I'll
sleep right and I promise you I'll be careful in
my travels. You both have taught me how to be
responsible and I won't forget what you taught.*

*I know you can't understand why I've gone
and done this to you. I never ever wanted in
my life to cause you to suffer and I just pray
you won't be too upset by me leaving. I would
just hate for you to be unhappy.*

*But God has called me to help this
preacher. I don't know why He chose me, but
I'm the one who got the job. I know you will
think it's all a bunch of foolishness, but
PLEASE just try to let me do this for God. I'm
different. You've known all along I was different. And I know you probably wished a thousand times I'd turned out some other way, but
I'm just like this and there's no changing me.*

*I just feel called. Like God has planted
some message in me and I've got to follow
what it says. And I can't do anything else till
I follow it.*

*So I've gone traveling with the Preacher.
He says he'll teach me things like I'd learn at
school, so you don't have to worry about that.*

And if he stops traveling and settles down someplace, then I'll start back to regular school.

I'll try to come and see you both when I can.

I'm asking you, please don't come after me or send the police to get me. We'll be hiding awhile, but I don't want to hide all my life. If you don't chase after me, I won't have to.

Just please don't worry. The Preacher will take care of everything. He's a GOOD MAN.

Mother, I wanted to leave you some kind of little present but I didn't have enough time to think up something real nice. So on my travels I'll look for just what I think you'd like and I'll send it to you.

Pop, I tried to finish up some work around the house. I would have painted the mailbox, too, but I ran out of paint. I'm sorry if I never did as much work for you as I could have. I really love you both. I wish I could take you with me. I'll be safe. Don't worry.

> Love,
> Pete

P.S. If you want, Rufus can have my bike. His is about busted.

When I finally woke up, the first thing I saw was the letter taped to my mirror where I'd left it. FOR MOTHER AND POP FROM PETE the envelope said. I'd borrowed some of Mother's pink-flowered stationery.

When I woke up, I saw the letter and, like in a dream, I got out of bed, walked over, and pulled the letter off the mirror, then climbed back under the sheet with it. I opened it up and, lying flat on my back, I read it. I read it straight through without ever yet thinking about what had happened the night before. I read it, I guess, to get some hold on everything that was spinning around in my head.

It was after eleven. Pop long gone. Mother probably out, too. The house quiet. The sun coming in the window.

I had slept like a dead person. And what happened to me at the filling station still wasn't coming through clear.

Dear Mother and Pop.

I really did write that letter yesterday, I thought. I really did write that letter and I really did pack my bag and I really did leave home last night. For good. I left home for good.

Then what was I doing lying in my own bed

the next morning? My letter in my hands and my duffel bag next to my bed and me supposed to be *somewhere else*?

Oh, Lord.

Where were you, Preacher? I waited and waited and you never came for me. Where were you?

I was all set. I was even early. I wouldn't even drink a pop, Preacher! I wouldn't even drink a pop because of you.

I watched that clock. You never came down that street, Preacher. You never came, then Rufus came. Rufus! And here I am with my insides all a wreck, and I am wondering, *Where are you, Preacher?*

Oh, that morning I hurt. I crushed up that letter to my folks and threw it across the room. I didn't want to get up but I didn't want to stay in bed, either. I didn't want to cry but I didn't want not to cry. I didn't want to remember but I didn't want to forget.

I just wished for some miracle.

I just wished for the Preacher to come walking in my door.

Deep down, I thought he would come walking in my door.

11

◆

The Messenger

"Pete?"

I tried to open my eyes but it was like they were zip-locked.

"Pete?"

I was hearing my name called, and as I came out of my dreaming I knew he had come back for me. I came out of my dreaming to find him.

I opened my eyes.

"Pete, you awake now?"

I looked at the face hanging over my bed, and I wanted to cry.

Rufus.

My mouth was all gummed together. "Water," I whispered.

Rufus gave me one of his annoyed looks, then went out. He came back with a bathroom cup full of water.

I sat up and drank it straight down. Then I sat rubbing my head, trying to come alive again.

"What time is it?" I asked.

"About noon."

"Grief," I said. I looked around me and spotted my duffel. Then I remembered it all, every bit, every single crystal-clear minute of it, and I wanted to roll back up in a ball and be alone.

"Thought I'd see how you're doing," Rufus said.

I remembered what he'd done for me, so I smiled a little.

"Fair," I answered. "Got enough sleep, that's for sure."

We were both quiet.

"Rufus, last night . . ."

"No problem. I was just passing that way and I saw you and . . ."

He was silent. We both knew lies wouldn't work with us.

"How long did you sit in those bushes?" I asked him.

"Long as you hung around that station."

I shook my head and sighed.

"Your folks weren't ticked off at you, staying out that late?"

Rufus grinned. "I told them I was going to spend the night with you. Which is kind of true, when you look at it." He thought a minute. "I just wanted to be there when you left town."

I nodded my head but I didn't smile anymore. I felt this big boulder growing in my stomach, pressing against my heart. I felt it so thick and heavy there, hurting and hurting.

"I don't know what happened to him," I whispered.

Rufus didn't say anything.

"I don't know why he hasn't come for me yet," I said. "Maybe he got in an accident. Or had a heart attack. I don't know what happened to him."

I looked at Rufus. And then I could see it. I could see it in his face.

Rufus knew.

Oh, I didn't want to ask him. I was afraid to find out, thinking I couldn't bear any more pain.

He was going to tell me the Preacher was dead. He was going to take away my Preacher.

"What?" I whispered.

Rufus opened his mouth to speak, then he shut it again.

"*What?*" I nearly yelled. I was sitting straight up in bed and I must have looked half-crazy.

"Pete," Rufus said. "Pete, I found out something this morning. It's buzzing all over town."

He paused. I thought I might break into a million splinters while I waited for him.

Rufus took a deep breath.

"Pete, he left town last night."

I stared at Rufus, waiting for things to clear up.

"He left town with Darlene Cook. You know. Homer Cook's big sister. The one who was a majorette last year and works at the drugstore."

I know my breathing just stopped cold.

My eyes got to watering, but I tightened them up. I wasn't going to let Rufus see me like that. I knew Rufus couldn't stand such stuff.

"When?" I whispered.

Rufus looked at me.

"After the revival. Darlene took off from her house about nine-thirty and—"

"No!" I yelled. I jumped out of bed, all my clothes still on me, even my shoes, and I kicked my duffel bag across the room. I heard the crack of something breaking inside.

"No!" I yelled again. I pointed at the door. "Get out! I don't want you here, Rufus! Get out of here!"

I never felt such a rage. And I wanted to throw Rufus out the window, I was so fed up with him. Rufus, always around, just always around and thinking he knew all the answers. Rufus who was always perfect and always right and always just *there*.

"Get out!"

Rufus was mad at me, too. I could see it in his face. His jaw was all tight and his eyes just glared. Rufus was strong. I figure he could have killed me if he wanted.

But he just gave me the sharpest, most cutting look I'd ever seen him give. Then he walked out and slammed my bedroom door shut behind him.

I stood there in the room, my body freezing up hard inside, and didn't know what to do.

I dropped to my knees.

"Help me," I whispered.

Then I stretched myself out on that floor and

cried like a baby. Cried the way I used to when Mother was going out the door. Seeing that door close.

He left with a girl. He left with a girl and me waiting for him.

I cried till I could cry no more. Then I just lay there on the floor.

Everything was so still. The sun was coming in hot through my window and it landed on my back and felt good. A bluejay carried on in the apple tree. And off down the street, I could hear the two Cornicelli kids, giggling and splashing in their baby pool.

He left me.

12

◆

The Light

I never knew life could be so hard.

I had never wanted to know anybody's secrets —not Mother's, not Pop's. *Don't tell me,* that's what I used to say.

I guess the secret I never wanted to find out was that life can be so hard.

And that people are not always what you think they are. Or what you want them to be.

Preacher Man never did come back. The story that went around town the rest of the summer was always changing, so I don't know what really happened. But Darlene Cook did take off with him that night. And most stories held that she left home about nine-thirty. Same as me.

Darlene had her own car, so they took off in that. One story said she left her car at a Greyhound station and they hopped a bus. But another story said she and the Preacher did all their traveling in the car and didn't take any buses—or hitchhike.

Darlene's folks had one big fit when they found out she was gone. Some said her father loaded up his rifle and set out on the road looking for her and the Preacher.

But everybody agreed there wasn't a thing he could have done, except maybe kill somebody. Darlene had graduated high school in May and she could do as she pleased.

Darlene was gone nearly three weeks. Then she came back home. And here's where all the speculation comes in. It seems Darlene wouldn't explain anything to anybody. She wouldn't say where she'd been those three weeks or what she'd been doing. And she wouldn't say one word about the Preacher. Not one word, good or bad.

So people in town took to making up their own stories. Some said the Preacher was the Devil in disguise and that Darlene found it out and came running back home. Others said the girl must have just cast a spell on the Preacher and it took him three weeks to shake it off and send her back. Some said Darlene probably thought she was going to have a baby. And then some said she probably wasn't with the Preacher at all, that she just wanted to have some fun out on her own and she made up a story about leaving town with him.

Well, nobody ever knew anything for sure. Nobody but Darlene. And I hear she still isn't talking.

The days after the Preacher left me were the darkest days I've ever known. Black days.

I wouldn't talk to anybody. I ignored Mother and Pop when I had to be around them, and I stayed in my room the rest of the time. Rufus didn't come back.

I guess I always believed hell was a pit of burning fire, like the middle of a volcano. I always believed it to be real, with red flames and all.

But hell is the only word I can think of to describe how I felt those days after the Preacher. Tormented. Hurt. And longing to cry out to God or to somebody, "Save me!"

I had been living my life trying my best to do right, to please God, so I wouldn't be sent into the fire. And never knowing that all it takes is one person, one earthly person, to put you there.

Maybe there really is a hell where people burn and burn. I just know one thing: If enough people do to me what the Preacher did, then if I do go to hell, I'll be used to it. I'll be ready for it.

Those were dark days. Days of emptiness and loneliness and loss of faith. Yes, I'd lost that, too.

I'd pray at night to the Lord, begging Him to change things. Mostly I asked to be with the Preacher again. Or I'd ask for the hurting inside me to stop. I'd ask to forget what happened to me.

But the next day nothing would be different. I'd just wake up and not want to get out of bed. And I'd ask myself what in the world was going to become of me, when the Lord wouldn't help me.

Mother and Pop were worried. They'd never seen me like that and I know they were watching me and secretly talking between themselves.

After about the fourth day of darkness, Mother tried to help me, to find out what was wrong. I was in my room that afternoon, lying on my bed, wanting nothing but to be with the Preacher, though by then I knew I hated him.

"Pete?" She knocked softly on the door, then came in carrying a basket of my clean clothes.

She didn't really look at me. And she walked into my room the way you'd walk into a doctor's office—when you're trying to be so quiet and trying to look cool when you're not.

She set the basket at the foot of my bed, hesitated a second, then said, "Peter, are you all right?"

"Uh-huh." I didn't bother to look at her.

"We've been worried about you, Pop and I. If there's anything we can do for you . . ."

I just shook my head.

She waited a minute, then started out the door. But as she was closing it behind her, without turning around to look at me, she said, "We love you, Pete."

And when the door closed, I wanted to cry again. But I didn't. I'd done enough crying.

Things stayed that way about a week or so. My folks left me alone, which not many folks would be good enough to do. But mine were different.

Yes, I guess if I learned one thing that summer, it was that I had a great mother and a great father. And not just because they left me alone when I needed it. There were other reasons.

Like, I *knew*, positively, that I could always count on them. Maybe their ideas about the world

were different from mine, but I knew they'd still
stick by me. And until the summer of the Preacher
Man, I never really thought about it. I guess I
just expected them to be like that.

But I know now that you can't expect anything
from anybody. If somebody loves you, it's because
he wants to. And it's never because it's what he's
supposed to do.

Don't expect anything. That's what I learned.

I never expected Rufus to forgive me for throwing him out of my room that day, either. I lost
the Preacher and I lost my best friend. I didn't
expect to get either one of them back.

So after that week of darkness, when the hurt
in me finally started to lighten up some and I felt
like getting out of the house, I went around town,
missing Rufus. I'd think how good it would be to
get a chili dog with him, maybe ride our bikes out
to the lake and take a swim. I'd even think how
good it would be to hear him say, "Hell, Pete."

Something else I learned: Not many friends in
the world were like Rufus. I sure missed him.

By the time Darlene came back to town, I'd
stopped being angry with the Preacher. I sure had
hated him for betraying me the way he did. But

even though I thought he could have handled things (me and Darlene) a lot better than he did, I wasn't mad at him.

I thought about going to talk to Darlene, too. But I couldn't risk it. Besides, it really wouldn't have changed anything for me. It wouldn't have taken away those dark days.

I did wonder, though, if God had a real purpose in allowing the Preacher to hurt me so much. Because, the way it turned out, I never knew about all the riches I had till the Preacher came into my life . . . and left it.

I've got to admit, I still worried about him. I worried he might be lonely. I figured he never wanted to hurt me or anybody else. I figured he just didn't know what to do about being lonely.

I still had Mother and Pop. And, before the summer was over, I had Rufus, too.

It was already August and I was mowing Mrs. Donaldson's lawn, just down the street from us, when Rufus rode by.

The mower was loud, so I couldn't have yelled at him if I wanted to. And I wanted to. I wanted to wave both my arms in the air and bring him back to me, smiling and cocky and saying, "Hey, you old hound dog!"

But I just watched him go by.

Then, before he was very far down the street, my mower ran out of gas. Just sputtered down and stopped. Everything was real quiet.

And I said, "Hell."

I didn't mean to. I still wasn't one for swearing.

But it just slipped out, and Rufus heard it.

He put on his brakes and he turned around and he looked at me like I was some creature from outer space.

Then his face burst into this big, wide grin and he chuckled, then he gurgled, and finally he just laughed out loud.

At first I just gawked at him. And I didn't know whether or not he was making fun of me.

But next thing I knew, I was giggling, too, and there we were, both of us, holding our stomachs and laughing our heads off. Him on his bike and me on the grass, laughing like hyenas.

Rufus and I made up that day. Somehow after the laughing was done, Rufus wheeled back to me and we got to talking. Then we went for a pop, and things were like they'd always been. Well, like they'd been before the Preacher came.

I still hadn't properly thanked Rufus for sticking by me that night I waited for the Preacher.

So before the summer was over, I used some of my mowing money and bought him a used guitar. He nearly hit me over the head with it because I spent my money on him. But he liked it a lot, and the first week he had it he learned to play "The Yellow Rose of Texas."

I also bought Mother and Pop something: That picture of the three of us—the one I took from the album when I was packing to leave—I got it blown up. And I bought a nice frame for it and hung it in the hallway, where you could see it if you were coming in the door, or going out. Even now, a year later and a year older, I never go through that door without looking at it.

◆

Amen

Rufus and I had a good time in eighth grade. He
made me go out for football with him, and after
the first day of practice I was so near dead, I
figured Rufus must want me gone so he could
finally have my bike.

But I didn't quit. And even though I didn't get
to play much during the season, I could sit right
out there on the bench and yell at Rufus to kill
them, and pound him on the back during time-
outs, and squirt some water down his throat before
he ran off again—and for those times, getting beat

up in practice was worth it. I'm even going to do it again this year.

Rufus and me, we had a good year. I also helped him pass English.

That summer of the Preacher Man just drew Rufus and me closer than ever before. And not because we were finally the same. Because we're not.

Rufus, he's still a hard-nosed atheist. He's a good, honest person—somebody I figure anybody could respect—but he still won't have any of that heaven talk.

And I won't try to change him. I'm hoping that's just something God will let slide.

Me, I still go to church sometimes. But it's a real quiet thing for me now. Sort of like a nice swim in a lake.

One thing I see now that I couldn't see last summer is that after the revival is over, the world is a place that isn't anything like the inside of a church on a hot summer night. It's a world where good guys like Rufus are happy atheists, and nice folks like my parents don't care much about church, and spiritual people like me. wander around on earth wishing it was heaven.

It's a world where somebody like the Man can

work so hard to save a million doomed sinners but come near killing the soul of one mixed-up kid. And never meaning to. I really believe that. He never meant to hurt me.

Is that what it's taken me a year to understand?

I've still got Mother and Pop. And Rufus. I know each one of them would walk through fire for me.

And I wonder, a year later, what the Preacher has got.

Maybe he'd say he's got the Lord. Maybe he'd say he doesn't need anybody else but the Lord.

Well, I do. I need Mother and Pop and Rufus with me.

Is that what's taken a year to understand?

But it still doesn't end there. Because even though I don't go to church as much—I'm still trying to figure church out—even though I don't seem to need church as much, I know I need God.

I just don't know how to get Him. And fit Him in with the other folks I need.

Maybe that's why I couldn't throw away these pieces of broken ceramic cross. The day I fished them out of my duffel, stuffed them in a paper bag, and put them in my drawer—that day, I thought it was the Preacher I was shoveling into the bag. Pieces of the Preacher. I wasn't ready to let go of him yet.

But now the pieces aren't him at all. They're me. They're me and God and all the powerful feelings I still have about Him. And I think now I can't throw away these pieces because they're a *cross*.

That's what finally needs finishing. The Preacher Man is behind me. But God is still right there, in front.

And just yesterday, just yesterday Rufus and I were sitting at the firehouse when I said, "Rufus?"

He said, "Huh?"

"You think you'll ever believe in God?"

"Doubt it."

"Well, you think *maybe*?"

"Maybe."

"That's good."

"Yeah, Pete," Rufus answered, "I know."

And, finally, I know, too. That throwing away this mess doesn't mean I'm giving something up. Or losing something I can't get back.

It's that there are too many pieces and too much dust.

I'm just ready for something whole.